D1408790

For Nicholas Christopher

This 1995 edition published by
Derrydale Books,
distributed by
Random House Value Publishing, Inc.
40 Engelhard Avenue, Avenel,
New Jersey 07001.

Random House
New York · Toronto · London · Sydney · Auckland

A CIP catalog record for this book
is available from
the Library of Congress.

Printed in China

ISBN 0-517-12120-4

MY BOOK OF
Nursery Rhymes

with pictures by
Caroline Crossland

DERRYDALE BOOKS
NEW YORK · AVENEL

GOOSEY GANDER

Goosey, goosey gander,
   Whither shall I wander?
Upstairs and downstairs
   And in my lady's chamber.
There I met an old man
   Who would not say his prayers,
I took him by the left leg
   And threw him down the stairs.

LITTLE MISS MUFFET

Little Miss Muffet
Sat on a tuffet,
Eating her curds and whey;
There came a big spider,
Who sat down beside her,
And frightened Miss Muffet away.

HICKORY, DICKORY, DOCK

Hickory, dickory, dock,
The mouse ran up the clock.
The clock struck one,
The mouse ran down,
Hickory, dickory, dock.

JACK AND JILL

Jack and Jill
  Went up the hill,
To fetch a pail of water;
  Jack fell down,
And broke his crown,
  And Jill came tumbling after.

SING A SONG OF SIXPENCE

Sing a song of sixpence,
  A pocket full of rye;
Four and twenty blackbirds,
  Baked in a pie.

When the pie was opened,
  The birds began to sing;
Was not that a dainty dish,
  To set before a king?

The king was in his counting-house,
　　Counting out his money;
The queen was in the parlour,
　　Eating bread and honey.

The maid was in the garden,
　　Hanging out the clothes,
When down came a blackbird
　　And pecked off her nose.

PUSSY CAT

Pussy cat, pussy cat,
   Where have you been?
I've been to London
   To look at the Queen.
Pussy cat, pussy cat,
   What did you there?
I frightened a little mouse
   Under her chair.

THIS LITTLE PIG

This little pig went to market,
  This little pig stayed at home,
This little pig had roast beef,
  This little pig had none,
And this little pig cried, Wee-wee-
  wee-wee-wee,
All the way home.

HUMPTY DUMPTY

Humpty Dumpty sat on a wall,
Humpty Dumpty had a great fall;
All the King's horses and all the King's men
Couldn't put Humpty together again.

MARY'S LAMB

Mary had a little lamb,
  Its fleece was white as snow;
And everywhere that Mary went
  The lamb was sure to go.

It followed her to school one day,
  Which was against the rule;
It made the children laugh and play
  To see a lamb at school.

THE OLD WOMAN IN A SHOE

There was an old woman
Who lived in a shoe,
She had so many children
She didn't know what to do.
She gave them some broth
Without any bread;
And whipped them all soundly,
And put them to bed.

THE CROOKED MAN

There was a crooked man,
  And he walked a crooked mile,
He found a crooked sixpence
  Against a crooked stile;
He bought a crooked cat,
  Which caught a crooked mouse,
And they all lived together
  In a little crooked house.

OLD KING COLE

Old King Cole
    Was a merry old soul,
And a merry old soul was he.
    He called for his pipe,
And he called for his bowl,
    And he called for his fiddlers three.

BOY BLUE

Little Boy Blue,
Come blow your horn,
The sheep's in the meadow,
The cow's in the corn.
Where is the boy
Who looks after the sheep?
He's under a haystack
Fast asleep.
Will you wake him?
No, not I,
For if I do,
He's sure to cry.

OLD MOTHER HUBBARD

Old Mother Hubbard
Went to the cupboard,
To fetch her poor dog a bone.
But when she got there
The cupboard was bare
And so the poor dog had none.

JACK HORNER

Little Jack Horner
Sat in the corner,
Eating a Christmas pie;
He put in his thumb,
And pulled out a plum,
And said, What a good boy am I!

THE CAT AND THE FIDDLE

Hey diddle, diddle,
   The cat and the fiddle,
The cow jumped over the moon;
   The little dog laughed
To see such fun,
   And the dish ran away with the spoon.

CONTRARY MARY

Mary, Mary, quite contrary,
How does your garden grow?
With silver bells and cockle shells,
And pretty maids all in a row.

LITTLE BO-PEEP

Little Bo-peep has lost her sheep,
And doesn't know where to find them;
Leave them alone, and they'll come home,
Bringing their tails behind them.

HUSH-A-BYE

Hush-a-bye, baby, on the tree top,
When the wind blows the cradle will rock;
When the bough breaks the cradle will fall,
Down will come baby, cradle, and all.

WILLIE WINKIE

Wee Willie Winkie runs through the town,
Upstairs and downstairs in his night-gown,
Rapping at the windows, crying through the lock,
Are the children all in bed, for now it's eight o'clock.